Valerie Thomas and Korky Paul

# Winnie the Witch

## Three Story Treasury

Winnie the Witch

Winnie Flies Again

Winnie in Winter

OXFORD
UNIVERSITY PRESS

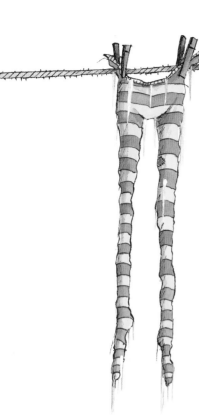

# OXFORD
UNIVERSITY PRESS

Great Clarendon Street, Oxford OX2 6DP

Oxford University Press is a department of the University of Oxford.
It furthers the University's objective of excellence in research, scholarship,
and education by publishing worldwide in
Oxford   New York

Auckland   Cape Town   Dar es Salaam   Hong Kong   Karachi
Kuala Lumpur   Madrid   Melbourne   Mexico City   Nairobi
New Delhi   Shanghai   Taipei   Toronto

With offices in

Argentina   Austria   Brazil   Chile   Czech Republic   France   Greece
Guatemala   Hungary   Italy   Japan Poland   Portugal   Singapore
South Korea   Switzerland   Thailand   Turkey   Ukraine   Vietnam

Oxford is a registered trade mark of Oxford University Press
in the UK and in certain other countries

This book first published 2007

Winnie the Witch first published 1987
Winnie in Winter first published 1996
Winnie Flies Again first published 1999

The stories are complete and unabridged

4  6  8  10  9  7  5  3

British Library Cataloguing in Publication Data
Data available

ISBN: 978-0-19-272727-5

Printed in Singapore

Paper used in the production of this book is a natural,
recyclable product made from wood grown in sustainable forests.
the manufacturing process conforms to the environmental
regulations of the country of origin.

www.korkypaul.com

# Winnie
## the Witch

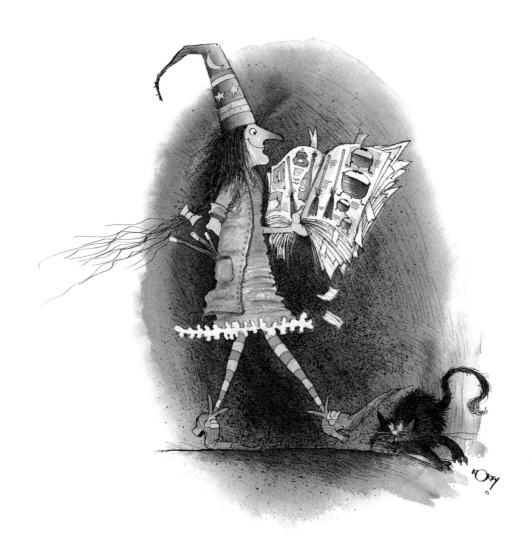

Winnie the Witch lived in a black
house in the forest.
The house was black on the
outside and black on the inside.
The carpets were black.
The chairs were black.
The bed was black and it had
black sheets and black blankets.
Even the bath was black.

Winnie lived in her black house with her cat, Wilbur.
He was black too. And that is how the trouble began.

When Wilbur sat on a chair with
his eyes open, Winnie could see him.
She could see his eyes, anyway.

But when Wilbur closed his eyes
and went to sleep, Winnie couldn't
see him at all. So she sat on him.

When Wilbur sat on the carpet with
his eyes open, Winnie could see him.
She could see his eyes, anyway.

But when Wilbur closed his
eyes and went to sleep,
Winnie couldn't see him at all.
So she tripped over him.

One day, after a nasty fall, Winnie decided something had to be done. She picked up her magic wand, waved it once and ABRACADABRA! Wilbur was a black cat no longer. He was bright green!

Now, when Wilbur slept on a chair, Winnie could see him.

When Wilbur slept on the floor, Winnie could see him.

And she could see him
when he slept on the bed.
But, Wilbur was not allowed
to sleep on the bed . . .

. . . so Winnie put
him outside.
Outside in
the grass.

Winnie came hurrying outside,
tripped over Wilbur,
turned three somersaults,
and fell into a rose bush.

When Wilbur sat outside in the grass,
Winnie couldn't see him, even when
his eyes were wide open.

This time, Winnie was furious.
She picked up her magic wand,
waved it five times and . . .

. . . ABRACADABRA! Wilbur had a
red head, a yellow body, a pink tail,
blue whiskers, and four purple legs.
But his eyes were still green.

Now, Winnie could see Wilbur when
he sat on a chair, when he lay on the
carpet, when he crawled into the grass.

And even when
he climbed to
the top of the
tallest tree.

Wilbur climbed to the top of the tallest tree to hide.
He looked ridiculous and he knew it.
Even the birds laughed at him.

Wilbur was miserable.
He stayed at the top
of the tree all day
and all night.

Next morning Wilbur
was still up the tree.
Winnie was worried.
She loved Wilbur
and hated him to
be miserable.

Then Winnie had an idea.
She waved her magic wand
and ABRACADABRA!
Wilbur was a black cat once more.
He came down from the tree, purring.

Then Winnie waved her wand again, and again, and again.

ABRACADABRA!

Now instead of a black house,
she had a yellow house with a
red roof and a red door.
The chairs were white with red
and white cushions. The carpet
was green with pink roses.

The bed was blue, with pink and
white sheets and pink blankets.
The bath was a gleaming white.

And now, Winnie can see Wilbur
no matter where he sits.

# Winnie
## Flies Again

Winnie the Witch always travelled by broomstick.
It was a wonderful way to travel.

Winnie would jump onto her broomstick.
Wilbur would jump onto her shoulder.
And they would zoom up into the sky.

There were no traffic lights.
No traffic jams.

Just the empty sky.

Well, that was how it used to be.
But, just lately, the sky had become
rather crowded.

Last week, Winnie didn't see a helicopter.
Wilbur lost two of his whiskers.

The week before that,
she didn't see a hang glider.

Wilbur's tail was bent.

The week before that, a very tall building suddenly got in her way.

Wilbur lost a clump of fur.

'The sky is too dangerous, Wilbur,' said Winnie.
'We'll have to try something else.'
So she took out her wand, waved it, and shouted,

ABRACADABRA!

Her broomstick turned into a
bicycle. But it was very slow.
Very hard to pedal.

And then a pond got in Winnie's way.
'She should look where she's going,' croaked a frog.

'A bicycle is worse than a broomstick, Wilbur,' said Winnie.
'We'll have to try something else.'
So she took out her wand, waved it, and shouted,

ABRACADABRA!

Her bicycle turned into a skateboard.
The skateboard was fast.
But it was hard to steer.
And impossible to stop.

Winnie was stopped. By an ice-cream seller.
'Can't you see where you're going?' he shouted.

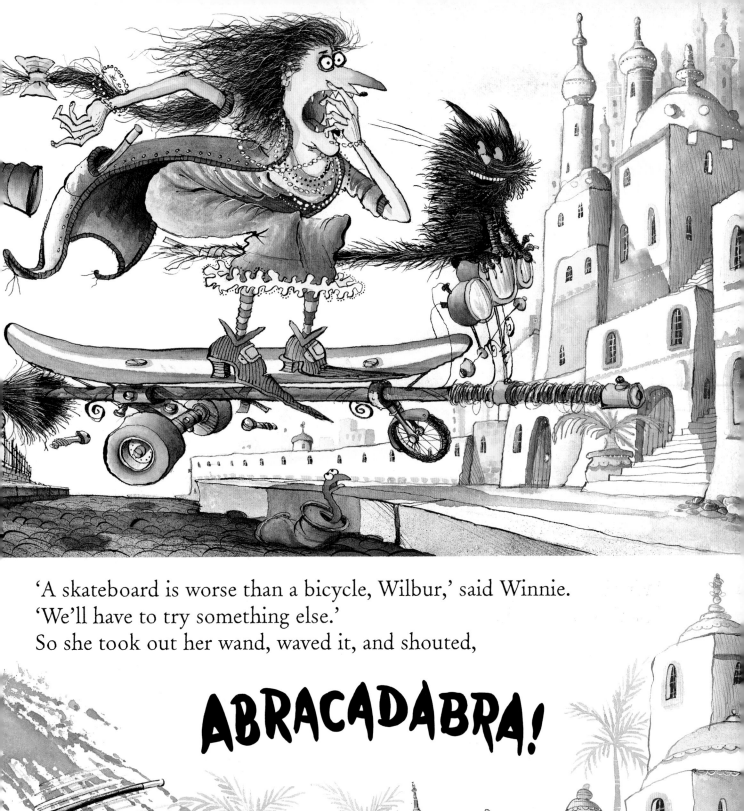

'A skateboard is worse than a bicycle, Wilbur,' said Winnie.
'We'll have to try something else.'
So she took out her wand, waved it, and shouted,

# ABRACADABRA!

Her skateboard turned into a horse,
and they trotted slowly down the path.
'This is much better than bicycles
or skateboards,' said Winnie.

But she didn't see . . .

. . . the low branch of a tree.
This time, Winnie didn't say anything.
She was hanging from a branch.

Slowly and carefully,
Winnie climbed down
from the tree.

'I think we'll walk
home, Wilbur,'
said Winnie.

They limped slowly along the road.
It was a very very slow way to travel.

But it was safe.

Until Winnie stepped into a hole
and tumbled deep down under the ground.

YES WE'RE OPEN

'I think I need a
cup of tea,' Winnie said.

Winnie climbed out of the tunnel
and went into a shop.

'A cup of tea and a muffin, please,' she said.
'And a saucer of milk for my cat.'

'We don't sell cups of tea or muffins,'
said the shop lady.
'And we don't have saucers of milk.
But I think I can help you.'

And she sold Winnie a pair of spectacles.

Now, Winnie and Wilbur travel everywhere by broomstick.
It's a wonderful way to travel.

# Winnie
## in Winter

Winnie the Witch looked out of her
window and shivered.
Her garden was covered in snow.
Her pond was covered in ice.
Icicles hung from roof tops.
'I'm tired of winter,' said Winnie.

Wilbur came in through the cat flap.
His feet were wet, and his whiskers
were frozen.
Wilbur was tired of winter, too.

Suddenly, Winnie had an idea.

She stopped what she was doing, took down her big book of spells, and read it carefully.

Then she put on her woolly coat, her fluffy hat, her snow boots, her gloves, and her scarf. She picked up her wand and she went outside.

Wilbur already had a fur coat on, so he went outside too. He thought something exciting might happen, and he wanted to watch.

Winnie shut her eyes.
Then she stood on tiptoe, counted
to ten, waved her wand five
times, and shouted,

ABRACADABRA!

And something magical happened!

Above Winnie's house the sun shone brightly.
The sky was deep blue.
All the snow had disappeared.
It was no longer winter at Winnie's house.
It was sunny summer.

Winnie took off her woolly coat, her fluffy
hat, her snow boots, her gloves, and her scarf.
She got her deckchair and went out in the
garden to sit in the sun.
'This is lovely,' said Winnie.
'Summer is much nicer.'

Wilbur lay down in the sun and purred.
This is lovely, he thought.
Summer is much nicer than winter.

All over the garden, little
animals were waking up.
They had been having
their winter sleep, and
they were very cross.

They came out into the garden,
yawning sleepily. 'It's too early
for summer,' they grumbled.
'We want to go back to sleep.'

The flowers had been asleep
under the snow. They woke
up and began to grow.
Up came the leaves,
and then the flowers.

But the sun was too hot
for them. Their heads began
to droop. All the lovely
flowers were dying.

Winnie was worried.
The animals and the flowers
didn't like her lovely summer.

Then she heard a very
strange noise . . .

Winnie turned around, and there behind her was a great crowd of people. They were running along the road towards her house.

They crowded into her garden.
They took off their coats, their
hats, their boots, their gloves,
and their scarves.

They sat in the sunshine.
They walked on Winnie's flowers.
They put orange peel on Winnie's
grass. They paddled in Winnie's pond.

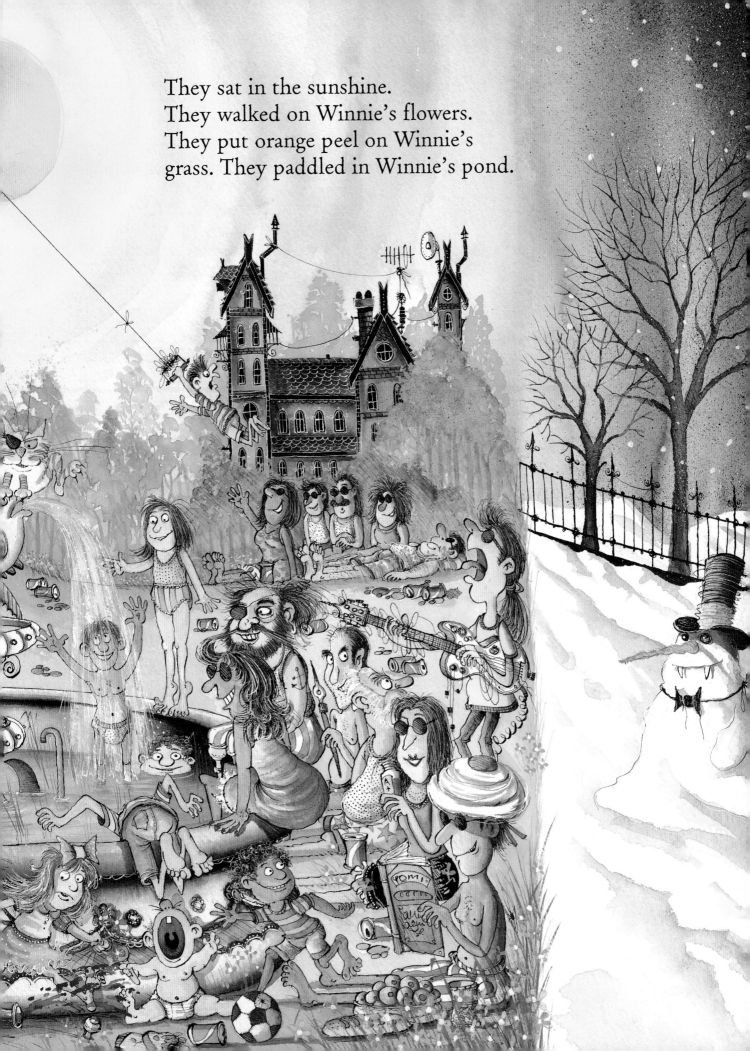

Soon there was no room for Winnie
and Wilbur in the garden. They went
inside and looked out of the window.
The noise was horrible.
The mess was horrible.
Winnie's lovely summer was horrible.

Then Winnie heard another strange noise.

A tinkling noise . . .

Somebody was selling ice creams in her garden.

Winnie was furious.
She grabbed her wand.
She rushed outside.
She stamped her foot, shut her eyes, counted
to ten, waved her wand five times and shouted,

# ABRACADABRA!

The sun disappeared.
The blue sky disappeared.
And the snow began to fall.

The people put on their coats, their hats, their boots,
their gloves, and their scarves, and rushed home.
The animals went back to bed, to finish their winter sleep.
The flowers went back under the ground to wait for spring.

Winnie and Wilbur went
back inside. Winnie made
a cup of hot chocolate and
toasted a muffin. Wilbur
had a saucer of warm milk.

Then Winnie snuggled into bed. Wilbur
curled up at the foot of the bed and purred.
'This is warm and cosy,' said Winnie.
'Winter is lovely too.'